THE LIZARD
JOSÉ SARAMAGO

WOODCUTS
J. BORGES

TRANSLATION
NICK CAISTOR & LUCIA CAISTOR

SEVEN STORIES PRESS
New York · Oakland · London

TRIANGLE SQUARE
books for young readers

This is a fairy tale.

Not that any fairies appear in it (nor did I say they did), but in what other kind of story would a lizard appear in Chiado?

Yes, one day a lizard appeared in Chiado. A big, green lizard, its eyes like black glass, its writhing body covered in scales, with a long, wavy tail and quick feet.

It stood there in the middle of the street, its mouth half-open, flicking its forked tongue, while the fine, white skin of its throat beat rhythmically.

It was a superb creature. Raised up on its back legs, as if to skitter off at any moment, it confronted passersby and automobiles. Fear all around. People and cars, everything came to a halt. Onlookers stood and watched from a distance. Some of the more nervous among them fled down side streets, pretending to themselves, in order not to admit their cowardice, that fatigue produces hallucinations, or so the doctor says.

Of course, the situation was untenable. A lizard standing there, a pallid crowd on the sidewalks, automobiles abandoned in neutral

—and suddenly an old woman shouting.

That was the last straw.

In the blink of an eye, the street was deserted.

The shopkeepers pulled down their shutters, a little girl selling violets (they were in season) dropped her basket and the flowers rolled over the ground, making a perfect ring around the lizard, like a perfumed garland.

The animal didn't move.

It slowly swished its tail and raised its triangular head, sniffing.

Somebody must have raised the alarm.

There was the sound of whistles; both ends of the street were blocked off.

At one end, firemen with all their equipment; at the other, soldiers fully outfitted.

Some said the lizard was poisonous, others that its scales were bulletproof.

The old woman was still shrieking, though no one knew where she was.

Panic filled the air.

A squadron of planes flew through the sky, observing, and down by Rossio could be heard the typical rumble of armored cars. The lizard took a few steps, breaking through the garland of violets.

The old woman was taken to the hospital in an ambulance.

This tale is almost at an end. We've reached the precise moment when the fairies intervene, although only indirectly. With all available forces assembled, the order was given to advance.

Fire hoses on one side, bayonets on the other,

And the thunder of the armored cars climbing the hill

—the all-out attack began.

From their windows, people gave advice and opinions from a safe distance. All against the lizard.

Suddenly the lizard (thanks to the fairies, don't forget) was transformed into a crimson rose, the color of blood, spread out on the black asphalt like a wound in the city.

Apprehensive, the attackers hesitated.

The rose grew, opened its petals, blossomed, perfumed the grimy house fronts.

In the hospital, the old lady asked: What happened?

Then the rose spun round, turned white, its petals became feathers and wings—and a dove took flight into the blue sky.

A story like this can only end in verse:

Silently, many remember,
In the prose of their houses,
The lizard that was a rose
The white rose with wings.

You don't believe me?

As I was saying:

fairies aren't what they used to be.

TRIANGLE SQUARE
books for young readers

an imprint of
SEVEN STORIES PRESS
140 Watts Street
New York, NY 10013
www.sevenstories.com

College professors and high school and middle school teachers may order free examination copies of Seven Stories Press titles.
To order, visit www.sevenstories.com or send a fax on school letterhead to (212) 226-1411.

LIBRARY OF CONGRESS CATALOGING-IN-PUBLICATION DATA

NAMES: Saramago, José, author. | Borges, J. (José), 1935– illustrator.
Caistor, Nick, translator. | Caistor, Lucia, translator.
TITLE: The lizard / José Saramago; woodcuts, J. Borges;
translation, Nick Caistor & Lucia Caistor.
DESCRIPTION: First edition. | New York, NY : Seven Stories Press, [2019]
Audience: Ages 6–9 | Audience: Grades 1-4 |
SUMMARY: "When a lizard appears in the neighborhood of Chiado,
in Lisbon, it surprises passers-by, and mobilizes firefighters
and the army"—Provided by publisher.
IDENTIFIERS: LCCN 2019023788 (print) | LCCN 2019023789 (ebook)
ISBN 9781609809331 (hardcover) | ISBN 9781609809348 (ebk)
SUBJECTS: CYAC: Lizards—Fiction. | Fear—Fiction.
Lisbon (Portugal)—Fiction. | Portugal—Fiction.
CLASSIFICATION: LCC PZ7.1.S2644 Liz 2019 (print)
LCC PZ7.1.S2644 (ebook) | DDC [E]—dc23
LC record available at https://lccn.loc.gov/2019023788
LC ebook record available at https://lccn.loc.gov/2019023789

Book design by Stewart Cauley and Abigail Miller

Printed in China.

9 8 7 6 5 4 3 2 1